How the Spider Became Bald

Folktales and Legends from West Africa

Peter Eric Adotey Addo

1993

**MORGAN
REYNOLDS
Incorporated**

Greensboro

HOW THE SPIDER BECAME BALD:
FOLKTALES AND LEGENDS FROM WEST AFRICA

Morgan Reynolds, Inc.
803 S. Elam Ave.
Greensboro, NC 27403 USA

Library of Congress Cataloging-in-Publication Data

Addo, Peter Eric Adotey, 1935-
   How the spider became bald: folktales and legends from West
Africa / Peter Eric Adotey Addo.
      p. cm.
   ISBN 1-883846-00-5 : $16.95. -- ISBN 1-883846-01-3   (pbk.) : $8.95
   1. Tales--Africa, West.   2. Legends--Africa, West.   3. Spiders-
-Africa, West--Folklore.   I. Title.
GR350.3.A33   1993
398.2'0966--dc20
                                                              93-30597
                                                                 CIP
                                                                 AC

Printed in the United States of America

First Edition

5 4 3 2 1

Dedication

To

my daughter

CHRISTINE AKU ADDO

Acknowledgements

My

sincere thanks and love
to my wife, Dr. Linda Addo,
for her invaluable help and support
during my work on the manuscript.

Contents

Introduction

The stories in this book are based on West African folktales in the oral tradition. Similar versions of the stories have been published elsewhere, but without preserving the qualities that make them African. A re-teller should always attempt to preserve the cultural nuances of the oral tradition that produced the original. Maintaining the original spirit of these stories has been my goal.

What are the folktales of Africa? African folktales deal with all life's cycles, rhythms, contradictions, and complexities. The folktales and fables are a gift from our ancestors. Short, often humorous, populated with heroes who never change, the stories were told when the sun had gone down and one could no longer work or play out of doors. Then, the young children would sit together around the fire to listen to the old people tell innumerable folktales. It was a favorite pastime,

along with drumming and dancing. The stories were repeated evening after evening. The children never tired of them, and, like children everywhere, wanted to hear them told with the exact words each time.

As previously mentioned, the folk tales are best when told in the vernacular idiom. Told in translation, they lose many of the jokes and puns, the funny twists of language, that the listener once enjoyed and anticipated eagerly. Translated tales have, for the most part, lost the special songs that were so much a part of them, especially for the Ghanaians. The song would be sung once or twice before the tale was begun. This had a double attraction: the children, curious to know whether the story was to be one of their favorites, could tell from the song which it would be; and very often the song told part of the story, ending abruptly at the most exciting point, and this sharpened the attention of the listeners, making them eager to know the end. But most stories heard today have lost all traces of the songs. They have been described as "Englished" folkstories. It is a great loss, but there is much to be valued and enjoyed in even these "streamlined" versions.

African folktales are first and foremost for entertainment. The stories are meant to be enjoyed, to create laughter and communion among the gathered listeners. The stories often instruct on the proper behavior of people who live in a community where proper social behavior is critical. The spider Ananse, the hero of many of these stories, often ends the tale exiled to the corner of the room, a just punishment for a character who puts his own wishes and desires before the needs of the community. The theme of many of the stories also reveals another verity of the community: the instinct of humans for knowledge is what brings wisdom. In one tale, Ananse collects all the knowledge in the world and tries to hide it in a gourd. His attempt is foiled, but it is the act of one who values knowledge and the wisdom it brings.

The way the old stories were told was important. The storyteller had to be both talented and skilled. One of the storyteller's goals was to instruct, and children are always inquisitive. This meant the storyteller must be capable of creating a story to answer any question a child may ask. If a child asked, "Why does the snake shed its skin?" the storyteller had to improvise an appealing and instructive story explaining the

natural phenomenon. The storyteller had a heavy responsibility: the most serious questions children ask were answered by folktales.

But the storyteller's aim was not only to reach the objective mind of the listener. The story must also reach the listener's inner self. The African folktale, like African sculpture, contains both the elegantly simple line that first catches the eye or ear, and volume or depth, which makes the story linger in the mind long after the storytelling is over.

The traditional tale from Ghana uses everyday activities to express life experience in a poetic way, to explain the way of life of the African people, the way of work, the ancestors, cultural aspirations, and even religious beliefs and philosophical perspective. There is enjoyment in these stories, and sadness, and wisdom. And while we may bemoan the passing of the culture that created these folktales, there is still much to be gained from their re-telling.

—REV. PETER ERIC ADOTEY ADDO
APRIL 28, 1993

1

How the Spider Became the Main Hero of Folktales

Long, long ago — yes, so long ago that the mind cannot actually imagine it — all folktales were about God. He was the hero who came to the aid of the weak and the poor. He was the superhuman who flew in the sky like a big eagle and bored in the ground like a squirrel. He was everything to everybody, and no story was ever told without mentioning His name. Every story was about Him and His deeds.

One day, as the story goes, Ananse the spider, being dissatisfied with the state of things as they were, thought it would be better if his name were used in the stories instead of God's name; and naturally he had to see God on this all-important matter. He went up to Wien, that is, the heavenly abode, and told God about

his wish. God replied, "If you, a spider, small as you are, want people to tell Ananse stories instead of God stories, you must prove that you have the same powers I have."

To prove his fitness to be the hero of all stories, the spider was given a task to do. He was given a grain of corn and was told to bring back to God a thousand men.

"This is an injustice," Ananse raged.

"It is my command," God replied.

"No person can perform such an impossible task," said the spider.

To this God replied, "Any person who is to be the hero of all stories must be able to perform this task easily. I command you to go and bring me the thousand men."

Upon such an imperative statement from God, the spider had no choice but to go and try.

First he came to earth, where people lived; and since he was tired, he went to an inn for the night. But before going to bed, he asked the innkeeper to guard the grain of corn with his life, as it belonged to God. The next morning it was discovered that the innkeeper's prize rooster had eaten the corn, and so the spider took

the rooster instead to show to God, despite the innkeeper's vehement protest.

The next day the spider found himself in another town. When the richest man here, who lived at the center of town in his very big compound, saw the prize rooster, he fell in love with it and offered to buy it, but the spider refused to sell it. Because night was coming on, the rich man offered the spider lodging. The spider accepted, but before turning in, he asked the rich man for a special safe place for the rooster, because it belonged to God and must be guarded, even with one's life.

The rich man put the rooster in a special pen where he usually kept his prize sheep, which were grazing in the fields overnight. It just happened that for some reason the sheep returned during the night; and they trampled upon and killed the prize rooster. The spider was furious when he discovered what had happened, and demanded compensation. The rich man, afraid because the rooster belonged to God, offered the one thing he prized above all his other possessions: he gave the spider his prize sheep. The sheep was to be taken to God in exchange for the rooster, with deepest apologies.

Two days later the spider arrived at the country of the cattlemen. Here he stayed at the house of the chief of all the cattlemen, asking him and his men to guard the prize sheep, which, according to the spider, belonged to God. But that night the cattle stampeded, and as luck would have it, the prize sheep happened to be in their path and was trampled to death. The spider refused to stay the rest of the night and insisted on taking the chief's prize cow to God in place of the sheep.

Because of the cow, the spider was slowed down considerably. In a few days, however, he reached the outskirts of a town, and meeting a funeral procession there, he inquired who had died. When told that the dead person was the only son of the poorest man in town, he offered to exchange the cow for the corpse. The family, being poor and knowing that the corpse had no value for them, gave it up willingly. When the spider arrived in the town, he went straight to the palace of the chief and asked for an audience at sunset.

When evening shadows were falling on the earth, the spider brought the corpse on a stretcher and informed the chief and his whole court that this was God's son, asleep because he was tired from the long

journey. He asked the chief for a room for God's son and a thousand men to guard him. Because up until then God was still the main hero of all stories and still ruled the earth, the chief was more than happy to comply. In fact, he took the request as an order and personally guaranteed and supervised the special room and the thousand men he provided to guard God's son, who was actually the corpse that the spider had brought with the prize cow, which he had gotten in exchange for the sheep, which he had gotten for the rooster, which he had gotten in exchange for the grain of corn that God had given him.

There was one little thing, said the spider, that the son of God demanded each time he went to bed, and that was a chicken. This was provided at once. But in the middle of the night the conniving spider, unknown to the thousand men, and under the pretense that he was going to say good night to the boy, went in, and after killing the chicken, smeared the corpse with its blood. The boy was found dead in the morning, and naturally the king's men were charged with negligence. The news of the son of God's death—or should we say murder?—spread throughout the land. Soon all the town came together in the chief's courtyard.

The chief was surprised beyond imagination when he found the boy dead. "Who has done this?" he demanded, but no one knew whom to blame for the crime. And because the victim was God's own son, the spider was more than angry. He was infuriated beyond description and spoke harshly of how he was going to tell God about what had happened. The chief, becoming frightened, called his council of elders together, and when the afternoon was over, they were still meeting. By nightfall they had reached a decision. They summoned the spider and invited him to choose anything in the kingdom to be taken to God in exchange for His son who had met with such an untimely and unfortunate demise.

After spending a considerable length of time in thinking over the chief's proposition, the spider asked to take to God the one thousand men who had been guarding over the boy during the night. The chief, his elders and the whole town were quite pleased with the spider's decision, and even provided the necessary transportation. They thought it good riddance to the thousand incompetent and cowardly men, anyway.

God was stunned and shocked when Ananse brought to him the one thousand men. And because

God had never been known to break any promise, He kept His part of the bargain and decreed that from then on His name should be dropped from all stories and only the spider's name should be used. The spider would be the main character in any story, and from that day the hero in all stories has been Ananse, the spider.

2

How the Spider Acquired His Two Extra Legs

The old people tell us that the spider is not like other insects. In fact, they do not place the spider in the family of insects, and there are several reasons for this. Among these are his greediness, cunning, and mischievousness, but most of all his extra two legs (as most insects have only six legs).

And the story is told how after the spider had won the honor of having his name in folktales, he still was not content, and so went back to ask God if He could make him a little different from all the other insects. According to the spider's argument, he had to be different, now that his name was featured in folktales.

It is said that God, the Great One above, was not impressed, and not convinced that He should yield to

the wishes of the spider. He remembered how the spider had outwitted Him, and brought Him the thousand men in exchange for just one grain of corn.

After giving great thought to the spider's request, God finally asked him what he wanted. The spider asked to have two extra legs, since all other insects had six legs. "That is almost an impossibility," said God. "But I am going to give you three tasks; and if you are able to fulfill them, two more legs will be given you, and you will be able to crawl upside down on walls, and you will not be an insect anymore. You will be removed from the family of insects into your own special family."

This sounded more than inviting to the pompous and clever spider, and so he asked for the tasks. Then God told him to bring to Him within a week the largest snake in the forest (the African black python), a pot of a million bees, and a lion.

Straightway the spider left the presence of God. He went home, and for days he racked his brain for a solution. His wife, Akonole, cooked his favorite dishes, but that did not cheer him up. His son, Kwakute, tried other ways but in vain, and even his daughter, Akonoleyawa, did not know what to do.

The third day the spider woke up very early and was about to go out, when Kwakute came and asked him why he was so quiet. "Well," said the spider, "I have asked God for two extra legs, but He has told me to bring the python, a pot of bees and a lion within a week. And I am going to obtain these things if it is the last thing I do." And with that he left the house.

The spider went into the forest and cut a long bamboo stick and went into the grass where the python lived. When he got there, he cut up some grass and made a rope out of it. It was time for the python to come out for food, and so the spider sat upright where the python was to appear and started saying to himself: "Oh, no! I tell you he is much much longer than this stick! . . . And I tell you I am right; he is not this long . . . No, he is—No, he is not—No, he is—No, he is not—No, he is . . ."

Just then the python came up and asked the spider with whom he was arguing and what in the world they were arguing about. "Well," said the spider, "it's my wife, Akonole. She said you are longer than this bamboo stick, and I told her that she was wrong."

"There is no need to argue," said the python, "because I know I am longer than this stick; so your wife Akonole is right."

"No, you are not," said the spider. "Don't think you can fool me, you midget of a python."

This wounded the python's pride, and he suggested that the spider use the bamboo stick to measure him, by placing the bamboo stick beside him. After the spider had done this, he said that the python was wiggling, and so the spider must tie him to the bamboo stick in order to measure him properly. When the python was thus tied up, the spider refused to untie him, over the loud protests of the victim. The spider took the python to God, and returned for his two other tasks.

For his second task the spider acquired a very large *calabash* (a gourd container taken from the calabash tree), and went into the grassland talking loudly to himself about the smallness of bees, and that all the bees in the world could not fill the gourd. This maddened the bees, and soon they were crowding into the calabash in swarms, to prove to the spider that they were not so small after all. When they were all inside, the spider sealed the calabash, to the astonishment of the bees, who protested in vain. He took the calabash to God, and returned for his last task.

The next task for the clever spider was to trap the lion. Now, the lion, being king of the forest and of all animals, was not going to be easy to trick, and the spider knew that. So he went into the forest with a very long and strong rope made out of sisal—the kind of rope the Ga people call *tankpee*, because it is the strongest.

Soon the two met, and the spider asked the lion his weight; and when the lion told him, the spider laughed so loud and so long that a large crowd gathered around. The spider told the lion that it was impossible for a lion to weigh that much because he, the spider, could easily lift a lion up. This angered the lion, because the spider was making a fool of him in public.

But, seeing the lion was angry, the spider continued, "And I am sure I can lift you in a bundle with just one hand."

Well, that did it. The lion replied that he could lift the spider up in a bundle with only one finger. "No, you can't," said the spider.

"Oh, yes I can!" replied the lion, "and if you want proof, here you are." The lion continued, "You have a rope. Let me tie you up, and I'll lift you up with just

one finger." This he did in no time, and then he challenged the spider to do the same.

Well, that was exactly what the spider was waiting for; and after getting the lion all tied up in a bundle, he refused to untie him. The spider then took the lion up to God, and he was given his extra two legs.

But when he got home, the other animals thought it was queer to have eight legs, and they laughed at the spider and made so much fun of him that he could not do anything but hide in the corners of houses for fear that he would be laughed at. And even up to now, though the spider can spin and build webs with eight legs and even walk upside down on walls, he just stays up at the corners of rooms and seldom comes down, for fear of being ridiculed.

The old folks say also that this is why everyone should be satisfied with what he has from the beginning. And there is a lot of truth to that, as you can see.

3

Why the Spider Is Usually Found
At the Corners of Rooms

A long time ago the spider and his family thought of going into the farming business. They decided to raise cash crops for sale; but later they changed their plan and raised yams instead.

Now, the only weakness of the spider was his love for yams. It was said that he loved yams so much that he once ventured into the northern territories where the lions lived in order to obtain them. In short, the spider's love for yams was legendary, and many tales were told of him and his yam addiction.

As was the custom in those days, all the members of the spider's family helped in the farm work, and naturally all of them would share in the benefits from the crops raised. This particular year the rains came in

at the right time, the yams grew wonderfully well, and the farm was the envy of all who saw it. The spider's family, his wife Akonole, his son Kwakute and his daughter Akonoleyawa were very proud, and they all looked forward with joy to the harvest.

But just before the harvest the strangest thing happened. The spider called his whole family together, at an early hour of the morning, as was the custom, because anything said at this hour was taken seriously. This was the hour of the morning when wife and husband usually had heart-to-heart talks, and father and son had manly talks, and mother and daughter came to grips with the facts of life. This hour of the morning was respected by all people because, it was said, the departed souls walked the earth at that time and therefore witnessed such talks.

After assembling his family, the spider asked them a favor. He requested that upon his death, they bury him in the middle of their farm, with the provision that the coffin should not be nailed and the grave should be left open. He further requested that they provide around the grave all cooking pots used in the kitchen and all his favorite herbs and spices. This was indeed a strange request, but at such an hour anything was taken

as sacred and any agreement was binding.

Soon afterward the spider took sick and suddenly died. Naturally the family was grieved at losing the father, but the saddest thing was that the spider hadn't lived long enough to enjoy the fruits of his labors in the yam field. They executed his last requests with all the solemnity that the occasion demanded, and even those who thought them odd were obliged to respect the dead spider's wishes.

After the funeral, the family noticed that a few yam plants were missing each day when they visited the farm. This was especially disturbing because they had not yet even tasted any of the yams. They were waiting for the natural harvest, when all the farmers harvested their crops together.

By chance, Kwakute, the spider's son, noticed that each morning it looked as if the pots around his father's grave had been used. It was of course singular for the dead to use pots, though the dead had on occasion been known to return, sometimes for revenge. But the spider had no reason to return. The son therefore devised a plan. He went out and made a large, man-sized doll and painted it with birdlime, the sticky material that children

used to trap birds and squirrels in the forest. He placed this doll in the center of the farm.

During the night, as had now become his daily routine, the supposedly dead spider came out of his grave and was about to set to work to fix himself a meal, when he saw a man standing in the middle of the farm. Naturally, he never expected anybody there at that time, so he asked in a loud voice who it was; but there was no answer. He thought the person was just playing a silent game, so he said again, "Who are you standing there?" There was still no answer; so he moved closer and said, "If you don't tell me who you are and what you are doing here, I'll slap you." Again there was no answer, so he slapped the doll, and his hand got caught on the birdlime. Then he slapped with the other hand, and that one too got caught.

Now the spider was angry as lightning, and he began to fight the doll, unaware that he was becoming entangled in the slimy, thick gum; and when finally he realized he had been taken in by a dumb doll, he was literally hanging on, just as lizards do on the walls of houses.

The next morning his family came, saw that he was indeed not dead, and removed him from the

gum. But the spider was so ashamed and so disgraced by the incident that he ran away and hid himself. And even when he came back home, he was never the same person again. He hid himself in the corner of his room and never came out unless forced by fire or his wife's cleaning. And to this day, one can still see the spider hanging up there, facing the wall in the corner of a room.

4

Greediness
Doesn't Pay

In the land of the spider and all his kin there was usually enough to eat, and there was a special kind of love among families, friends and relatives. People loved one another so much that they shared their belongings with those who were in want. All families were at peace, and when a family did not have enough harvest from a crop, naturally the other families pitched in to help. There was such peace and such good relations among all the people, that the land was referred to as the Land of Tranquility.

As time went on, there was suddenly a great famine in the land, so severe that many people died of starvation, and those who remained became as thin as bamboo sticks and only waited for death to come. The

rains had stopped, and so the crops had failed. Food became so scarce that even the other animals left or perished. The famine was so sudden that no preparations could be made, and everybody suffered one way or another. The sea yielded up no fish for the fishermen and the forest no game for the hunters.

And so it was that each day the spider went out in search for food for himself and his family. They were so hungry they could have eaten the ashes from the fire that was made to cook the food that was never available. One day, as by now had become his habit, the spider went aimlessly walking, and eventually he got to the beach. He sat down for a while and looked at the blue sea and watched the waves forming whitecaps as they neared the shore. He saw a lot of seaweed, but it was all dried up and the beach was as bare as his stomach. After sitting on the sand for a while, he got up to walk in the surf along the beach. As he walked he saw a very beautiful pebble, and he started to kick it; but because it was so beautiful and he had nothing else to do, he picked it up, and said to himself, "What a beautiful pebble! I'll take it and hold it under my tongue to keep me from biting my tongue, for I'm terribly hungry."

Just then the pebble said, "I am the one who shakes, and I can shake anything out of me."

Well, thought the spider, that was ridiculous—a talking pebble—and he was about to throw the pebble away, for he must be hearing or imagining things and it was high time he got hold of himself. Hunger makes one see, do and even hear strange things. Just then the pebble said, "If you don't believe me, simply say 'shake, pebble shake'. These words are magic, and when you say them to me, I will shake out anything you desire. But then, after you are satisfied, you must say 'stop, pebble, stop', and I will stop."

Now the spider became curious and took an interest in the pebble. He was sure now that he was not dreaming, or anything stupid like that. So he said, "All right, if you are the one who shakes, then 'shake, pebble, shake'. Shake out for me a favorite dish, which is rice and lamb stew." Actually, he was too famished to realize what he was saying. Suddenly the spider felt the pebble moving in his hand. He threw it onto the sand, and then the most remarkable thing happened. Right in front of him was his favorite dish— rice and lamb stew. He at first thought it was a mirage. "What a funny dream!" he said. But then he touched it,

and smelled it; then he was sure it was real. What a day! The spider ate to his heart's content, and then said "'Stop, pebble, stop', for I have had enough." He then took the pebble home in order to give his family some food also.

But on his way home, he reflected how stupid it would be if he went along with the notion of sharing the powers of the pebble with his family and friends. After all, it was he who had found it. He said to himself, "Who knows? The food in this pebble might not be enough for both me and my family." By the time he got home he had made up his mind to tell no one about the magic pebble. Instead, he hid the pebble under his bed, and from then on he fed himself from it each night when his family were all asleep.

Soon, people began to notice a distinct change in the health and looks of the spider. He seemed to be gaining weight, and for some reason he was happier. He walked straight and did not show the usual signs of the hunger that had crippled the land and the people. This was mystifying; and it suddenly occurred to Kwakute, the spider's son (who knew how cunning and sometimes greedy and sneaky his father was) that something must be amiss. He took to following his father around secretly

and did not let him out of his sight at any moment. That same day, Kwakute's suspicions were verified.

As usual, when the spider became hungry, he went into his room and locked the door. But as the saying goes, a sneaky father always has a sneakier son. Thus, unknown to the father, the son was watching through the keyhole. When the father had finished feeding himself, he left as usual under the pretense of searching for food. After the father had left, the son called in the whole family, and using the magic words he had heard, he commanded the pebble to shake out all sorts of food for them.

That day was bigger and better than any festival day, because when the word went around that there was food in the spider's house, people came from everywhere to eat and rejoice. The only fly in the ointment was that the son forgot to say "Stop, pebble, stop" even when the house was overflowing, and the pebble kept right on issuing out food. So it kept on, until far into the night, to the enjoyment of all the people. Finally, though, the pebble simply ran out of food. It was all used up.

The spider naturally was outraged and seething when he came home and found out what had happened. But there was nothing in the world he could do, for he

was carried shoulder-high as a hero who had brought food to save the people. Inside of him, though, he knew the truth.

The famine continued, and soon starvation and death set in again. Once again the spider kept up his daily search for food, only to come home empty-handed. He even went back to the beach where he had found the magic pebble, just in case there was another. But he talked himself blue in the face failing to invoke a response from the pebbles on the beach.

One day on his way home from his search he passed through a thick forest. He was tuckered out, and sat down on a log to rest. As he sat, he picked up a stick to drive away an ant that tried to crawl on him. Then he heard the strangest voice. That is, he thought he heard a voice. But that was impossible; the place where he sat was not generally frequented by people. But, since his experience with the magic pebble, he had developed a habit of talking to anything and everything. So he said casually, "Now, stick, don't tell me you can talk."

A voice answered, "Oh, yes I can!" To his astonishment the stick went on, "Oh, yes—you're right, I can talk. My name is Whip. I can whip anything for you, or anyone."

Now the spider could not control himself, and he retorted, "Okay. If you can whip, whip anything— even me."

The spider was flabbergasted when immediately he got a good beating from the whip. When the spider cried "Stop, whip, stop!" the whip fell from his hand. He was about to run away and leave the stick behind, when a thought occurred to him: he would teach his family a lesson. So he took the stick home, and hid it under his bed. Since by this time every move he made at home was being watched by his son, he pretended to be busy in his bedroom. He then came out and left the house.

After he had left, Kwakute went in and found not a pebble, as before, but a whip. The family examined it but did not know what to make of it. "It looks like an ordinary stick to me," said one.

"It looks like a whip," said another.

Then the voice of the spider's wife, Akonole, was heard. She said, "If it is a whip, ask it to whip something." Actually she said it as a joke. But to the dismay of everyone, that was the magic phrase; and soon pandemonium set in. The whip went on to whip them until they were sore; and as they did not know the

magic words to stop the whip, it kept on until the spider arrived and stopped it.

It was a great lesson, and from that day no son has ever spied on his father, and the spider himself has always shared with his kinfolk. He learned that greediness doesn't pay, ever!

5

The Spider and the Monkey

Once the spider awoke and discovered he had no money at all. He searched everywhere but could not find any money. You see, he had played so much that he had not worked for a long time. He laughed at the other animals as they passed by his house on their way to work. They usually greeted him, and he would mumble how sad it was for them to have to get up so early to find work and food.

Well, this went on for a long time, until the spider thought of a scheme. One morning he asked the monkey to stop by, and told him he had discovered a special medicine to cure his nervousness, for which the spider demanded a sum of money. He explained that he was venturing into a new business. The monkey

believed him, because the spider guaranteed the cure or his money back after forty days, the usual number of days a family mourned a death.

Of course, the medicine did not work. After forty days, knowing that he owed the monkey his money back, the spider tried to come up with a plan to repay the loan. (It did not take him very long. Some say his head is full of tricks.) First he invited the lion—the most feared in the forest—to his home for dinner. He asked the lion to come exactly at noon, when the sun is highest in the sky.

At the same time, he promised the monkey he would be home early in the morning, so that the monkey could come and collect his money. Then the spider asked his son Kwakute to stay home to warmly receive the monkey, and to ask him to stop and visit. "Tell the monkey I will return shortly, and we will have dinner in the mango tree. Have him wait there for me." After giving his son Kwakute the instructions, the spider pretended to leave. But actually, he hid, so he could watch the events at his house.

The monkey came by as scheduled, and was happy to wait in the mango tree. The spider, hiding close by, could barely contain his laughter.

At noon the lion approached, roaring for the food the spider had promised. Ananse, however, shouted to him: "Look up, you fool. Your dinner is in the tall mango tree."

As the frightened monkey tried to climb down, the mighty lion, thinking the monkey was his dinner, tried to capture him. But the fast-moving monkey escaped. The lion chased after him, and it is said by the wise old people who know, that to this day the lion still chases the monkey for his dinner.

6

How the Spider
Became Bald

Once upon a time the spider, above all the other animals, was known to have the most beautiful hair. He had hair all over his body, including his head. It kept him warm during the night, and it was his great pride.

One day the spider went to visit his mother-in-law in the next city. She was always nice to her sons-in-law and daughters-in-law, and the spider was no exception. The spider had travelled all day, and he was tired and hungry. Naturally the mother-in-law offered him some porridge to eat, but he was so shy that he refused it. (It's hard to believe, but the spider was once very shy and humble.) After a while he was again offered some food, but again he refused. Then, when he was about to leave, the mother-in-law offered to walk him out of

the house, and she went to put on a coat. Quickly the hungry spider took some of the steaming porridge, which is more or less like mashed potatoes, and was about to eat it, when the mother-in-law reappeared. He hurriedly dumped the hot porridge in his hat and then put the hat on his head, and when his mother-in-law asked why he was shaking his head, he told her that he was doing a new kind of dance called Shake Your Head. But the food kept burning him, until he couldn't stand it any longer. By that time his mother-in-law realized what was happening, but the damage had been done. The heat had burned the spider's scalp, and made him bald.

This was more than he could stand, and he ran away in disgrace. And up to now he has not come back. But people often report seeing him hiding up in the attic or at the corner of a room. And even today, if you look closely you will find no hair—or very little of it—on the spider's head.

7

Why the Snake
Sheds Its Skin

When God the creator of all living things in the forest made each animal he gave to each special qualities. To the rabbit, he gave the ability to run fast and to smell anything from a mile away. To the spider, God gave extreme intelligence. To the monkey, the Creator gave the ability to scratch but not beauty. Some say even today that the average monkey is still trying to improve on his face, thus the constant moving. But the old wise ones claim that the Creator just gave the monkey nervousness—for what reason no one knows.

And so it was. Each animal had its own special attributes, and were satisfied. Well, that is, until the spider looked around and realized all he had was the ability to walk on eight legs. He was not

satisfied just with that, so he developed a plan to obtain some other traits.

According to the story, long ago the snake came in many colors like a chameleon. He kept his skin smooth by moving gently among the fallen leaves that form a thick carpet on the forest floor.

One day on the snake's journey through the forest, he came upon the spider who looked as if he had been beaten and then left beside a tree trunk. The snake, not suspecting anything, stopped to offer help.

As the story goes, the spider, pretending to be weak and cold, started moaning about how a robber had taken his *kente* cloth, which everyone knows is multi-colored, handwoven, and expensive. The spider was on his way to a special festival and was wearing the beautiful *kente* cloth, but his attacker had taken it and left him beaten and bruised.

The snake naturally felt sorry for the spider, but did not know what to offer except his sympathy. But sympathy was not what the spider wanted. He had planned the meeting to trick the snake into giving him his special skin, so he could wear it. You see at that time the snake did not know that he could part with his skin.

Well, after a few hints from the shivering spider, the snake agreed to try to help by shedding his skin in order to cover the spider and keep him warm. He asked the spider to hold his tail; and, slowly, he realized he could wiggle through, and that the skin shedding did not hurt him. The spider, however, was sure that the act of shedding his skin would kill the snake, and in fact had planned to take the snake home as his dinner. But the snake wiggled away, and the spider discovered when he got home with the snake's discarded skin that it had lost all of its sheen and color.

Surpisingly, once out of his old skin, the snake began to grow and grow. As he grew larger, the other animals, like rabbits and rats, became afraid of the larger snake, who took advantage of every opportunity to swallow them in one gulp. Although the other animals were afraid, the snake was happy, because what the spider thought would harm him had turned out to be good for him. And now, anytime the snake feels himself growing fat from eating the other animals, and his skin becomes a little tight, off goes the old skin. It makes sense.

8

How Wisdom Again Became Common to All

I t is generally said that it was only by a nasty fall that wisdom became common to people again. And this was due to the greedy instincts of the spider.

Wisdom was once common to all; all people had wisdom. This situation did not sit well with the spider; so he took the matter into his own hands to deprive everyone of their wisdom. He decided to collect all the wisdom on earth and to hide it in a pot on top of the silk-cotton tree, which is a giant among the trees of the forest. And there are thorns around the trunk of the tree, no man would ever be able to get to the pot of wisdom at the top.

But while the spider was climbing, he fell, and the pot of wisdom broke. And when the people came to

gather up their lost wisdom, the ones who came first took too much, and there was only a little left for those who came later. And that that is why though today all people still possess wisdom, only a few have a lot.

9

Why the Elders Say We Should Not Repeat Sleeping-Mat Confidences

I t is said that once upon a time Nyankopon, the sky god, cleared a very large farm and planted okras, onions, beans, garden eggs (eggplants), peppers and pumpkins. But the weeds in the garden grew up thickly as well, and many prickly, stinging nettles sprang up. So Nyankopon beat the gong-gong and made a proclamation to the effect that anyone who could weed his overgrown farm without having to stop and scratch himself, might come forward and take his daughter Abena, the ninth child, in marriage.

All the brave men came forward and tried to weed the sky god's garden. But all scratched themselves when the nettles tickled, and were laughed at because they failed.

The spider, clever as he was, came to Nyankopon and said, "As for me, I am able." Now, Nyankopon's farm was situated on the side of a path, and that path was the one people would take going to the market every Friday. And the spider, being aware of this, made it a point to clear the weeds only on Fridays, and the reason was this: When he was hoeing, and the passers-by greeted him with, "Hail to you at your work, Father Spider!" he would answer, "Thank you, my friend."

Then the passer-by would say, "Why are you trying to clear this farm, when no one else has been able to?"

The spider would answer, "Ah, it's all because of the girl that I am wearing myself out like this. Do you know, her arms are so soft and lovely, not rough like mine," and here he would slap and rub his arm where it had begun to itch. And when he did so, he would get relief from the irritation. Then another walker would pass and hail him, and he would take his hand and slap another place that was itching. For example, if his thigh itched, he would say, "That girl of mine! Her thigh is so lovely, not at all like my ugly thigh here," and he would slap and rub his

own thigh. In this manner, he finished clearing the plantation.

Then he went off to tell Nyankopon. Nyankopon asked his aides, "Has he really finished?"

The aides said, "Yes."

Then Nyankopon asked them, "Did he scratch himself?"

They said, "No, he did not scratch himself."

Then Nyankopon took Abena and gave her to the spider.

One night, not long after, the spider and his bride went to bed, and Abena asked him, "How is it that you of all people were able to clear my father's farm, a farm which all the brave men could not weed?"

The spider said, "Do you suppose that I am a fool? I kept clearing, and when anyone passed by and asked me, 'Kwaku, [that was the spider's first name], why are you clearing this farm, which no one else has been able to clear?' I would slap any place on my skin that was itching me, and scratch it in that way, and declare to the person that, for example, your thigh was beautiful and polished. That was how I was able to weed it."

Thereupon Abena said, "Aieee! Tomorrow I shall tell my father that you scratched yourself after all."

The spider said to her, "You must not mention what I have said, for this is a sleeping-mat confidence."

Abena said, "I know nothing about sleeping-mat confidences, and I shall tell the truth tomorrow." Then Abena took her sleeping-mat away from beside the spider and went to lay down at the other end of the room.

Now the spider's eyes grew red; and he went and took his musical bow and he struck the string and sang a sad song: "I told Abena, the ninth child, this is not a matter about which to quarrel. Let us treat it as a sleeping-mat confidence. But she said No. She has a case against me now; ah, but someone else also has a case, and is already walking down the road. I know that, but she does not know yet."

After a while the spider got up and called to his wife Abena, but she was fast asleep. Then the spider said, "I've got you," and he took some water and poured it over Abena's sleeping mat. Then he went to bed, but not to sleep.

After a while he got back up and woke Abena, and said, "Wife, what is this? You have wet the sleeping mat, you shameless woman. Surely you are not at all nice. In the morning I shall tell everyone. It was true what

they all whispered—that you wet your bed. A wife who wets her bed!"

Abena said to him, "I implore you, please do not tell anyone. Let the matter drop."

The spider said, "I will not let it drop. You said you would tell your father that I scratched, and I asked you not to, but you said No. Because of that I will not drop the case."

And Abena said to the spider, "If you drop my case, I shall drop yours and none shall know our confidences, for if you do not drop mine, I shall die of shame."

Then Ananse said, "I have heard. Since you so desire, let it be a sleeping-mat confidence. So the matter ends here." What Abena did not know was that the spider was actually laughing within himself and saying, "Abena, I have got you!"

And that is how the elders came to say, "Sleeping-mat confidences are not to be repeated." And even now, among the Ga people, anything said in the early morning hours in bed remains in confidence.

10

How the Spider Helped the Chief's Daughter to Regain Her Speech

Now the Chief of Kwaman had a beautiful daughter; and she was said to be the most beautiful girl in all the land. But when she was twelve, it was discovered that she could no longer talk. The chief called in all his priests and physicians, but none could make her talk. Therefore the chief sent out word that he would give half of Kwaman to anyone who would be able to help his daughter regain her speech.

An Okomfo came, but his powers were not able to help the girl. Then a Wulomo came, but he also could not help or do anything. All were hooted at. Even the Klote and Sakumo priests came and were hooted at. Many came to try, but failed, and they were hooted at.

Soon word was all around that the Chief of Kwaman's daughter was hopelessly mute.

Then one day the spider heard the news and came down to try to help the Kwaman chief's daughter regain her speech. He took the young girl to the river and asked her to fill a bucket with water, using a basket he gave her. The daughter went into the water and tried to take it up into the basket, but the water drained out before she could get to the bucket.

After several unsuccessful attempts, the spider came by with a long whip and threatened to use it on the girl if she were unable to fill the bucket. The spider then went to hide in the bushes and watched. After a while the girl was so disgusted that she burst out, "Only a stupid fool would try to use a basket to fill a bucket with water!"

The spider then jumped out and took the Chief of Kwaman's daughter home. When the incident was told, the spider was given his reward. From that day on the girl began to talk again, just like everybody else. As for the spider, no one knows what he did with his portion of Kwaman. Some say he sold it to the Ga people, and even now the people of Kwaman still claim that part of the Ga lands are rightfully theirs.

11

How the Spider Outwitted the Fox

O nce upon a time when all the animals lived together, humans lived close by, and the animals never feared them. Humans in turn welcomed all the animals of the forest into their homes. But of course this is not the case now. Most of the animals fear humans, and we find an inherent enmity between most humans and foxes particularly. Many reasons have been given for this, but among the Ga people the story is told in an interesting way.

It seems that the fox was once a friend of the spider, and both were very friendly to a man who lived not far away. And every time the fox and his friend the spider came out of the forest, the fox would make his usual howling noise and the man would come from the village to meet them.

One day the man took them back to his farm, which had many chickens pecking about. The always hungry fox wished he could have one of the chickens for lunch. The spider felt the same way, but he could control himself better than the fox, and he never did give any indication of wanting one of the man's chickens for lunch. As long as the fox and the spider stayed away from the chickens, the friendship between them and the man grew.

One day the spider went to see the man alone; but when he got to the house, there was no one in. He knocked and knocked, but no one answered. Behind the house he could hear the chickens, and all of a sudden his mouth watered. The saliva flowed down his chin—as if, the Ga people say, he were an idiot. He turned to go away, when a thought occurred to him. "Why," he said to himself, "the man is not home, and no one here would know if I took just a couple of his chickens." So the spider went to the yard and helped himself to as many chickens as he could. And just as he had surmised, no one saw him. He took the chickens home and had a wonderful dinner that night.

But what the spider had not figured out was how to dispose of the chicken feathers. As the saying goes,

smoke is produced only by fire. If, he thought, anybody saw the feathers, it would mark him as the chicken thief; moreover, this would break the friendship between him and the man.

That night the fox met the spider carrying a great big heavy sack that weighed him down. He could scarcely carry it, and was struggling to do so. The fox hailed him and asked what he was carrying in the sack. "Oh, nothing," said the spider. But the fox knew how sneaky the spider was, and followed him and demanded to know. He kept it up and refused to leave until the spider told him what he was carrying. "Well," said the spider at last, "you will regret this, but I am going to tell you. I am carrying *ma*," (the corn dough used for making *banku*, the staple food of the Ga people). "And not only that, but the sack contains *kpinloo*" (the best meat used by the Ga people to make groundnut, or peanut-butter soup)." The fox could not contain himself and begged for some of the meat.

"Well," said the smart and alert spider, "if you would carry the sack for me, I would let you have some of the meat." And so the fox agreed to carry the sack. The spider sat down under a nim tree to rest and told the fox he was going to catch up to him after a while.

A few minutes later the man passed by, and seeing the spider under the nim tree, asked him what was the matter. "Nothing is the matter," said the spider. "I have just been sitting here and wondering if the sack carried by the fox over there doesn't contain some feathers."

"Feathers!" shouted the man, for he knew feathers would mean someone had been to his chicken farm.

He ran to catch up to the fox, and when he asked him what was in the sack, the fox replied, "*Kpinloo*." He asked again and the fox said, "Well, *ma* for banku, and *kpinloo* for the soup, which the spider sitting over there gave to me just a moment ago." By this time a crowd had gathered, and they demanded to see what it was the fox was carrying. It was then that the man opened the sack. And what did he find? The sack was full of chicken feathers.

The fox was astonished, but the man was angry. He took out his knife and chased the fox. The fox ran off without looking back, and so it has been till now. The fox hides from the man, and the man is always on the watch for the fox. The fox has devised all manner of ways to escape him, yet the man persists without getting tired. The moral of the story is that one should not carry a sack without knowing the contents.

12

How the Spider Paid His Debts

One day the spider realized that he had contracted a great number of debts. In fact, he had borrowed from every animal in the forest; and he took counsel with himself as to what he should do, for he had no money with which to pay. Then he sent word to all his creditors to meet him on a certain Friday so that he could pay them.

When the Friday came, and while it was still early in the morning, the hen arrived to collect her debt. And when she came, the spider said, "Good, I will pay at once; but wait a minute or two while I prepare you some food." So the hen waited inside the hut while the spider went outside.

Soon the cat came. The spider said to him, "Good. The repayment is in the hut," and so the cat went and

entered the hut and seized the hen and twisted her neck.

Just as the cat was about to go away, the dog arrived, and the spider said, "Good. The repayment is in the hut; go and take it." So the dog went in and seized the cat and killed him.

Just as the dog was about to go, the hyena arrived; and the spider said, "Good. The repayment is in the hut; go in and take it." So the hyena ran in and seized the dog and ate him.

Just as the hyena was about to leave, the leopard appeared; and the spider said, "Good. The repayment is in the hut; go and take it." So the leopard sprang upon the hyena and killed him.

Just as the leopard was about to leave the lion arrived; and when he saw his enemy the leopard, they began to fight. While they were fighting, the spider took some pepper and sprinkled it in their eyes. After that he took up a big stick and beat them until they were both dead. Then the spider and his family collected the meat and had a great feast.

13

The Spider
and the Fox

O nce upon a time the spider challenged the fox to a race. Before the day appointed for the contest, the spider entered into league with all his companions and arranged that they should station themselves at regular intervals along the course.

As soon as the race started, the fox began outstripping the spider with ease, and he called back in mocking tones to ask where the spider was. To his surprise, the answer "Here I am" came from in front of him, the opposite direction to what he expected. He was startled, and raced along once more, and repeated the challenge. Again a voice answered from in front of him, and once more he was deceived into thinking that he was being left behind in the race. The strategy was

repeated all along the course, until the fox fell exhausted and could not finish. The spider then dashed forward and won the race. This made the fox angry. To this very day, he has been looking for the spider; but the spider hides himself in the nooks and crannies out of the path of the fox, because he knows what is in store for him if he should ever be found.

14

Why the Spider's Body is Divided Into Three Parts

Do you know that the spider's body was once in one piece? Some people claim that was why he could go through tight spots and hide away in a crack in the trunk of a tree.

The spider used to boast of how straight and slim his body was built, and how he could hide in unexpected places to listen to what all the animals were saying. In fact, the spider often bragged that he knew everything that was going on, and he made it his duty to listen to what every animal had to say, in secret or not.

One day, as the story goes, the spider heard that there was going to be a big festival somewhere in the forest, but he did not know where. And so he called

in his twin sons, Akwete and Akuete. Akwete was a clumsy boy, who often fell down. Akuete was very nervous, and liked music and dancing more than anything else in the world.

Now, of course the spider could spin out strong, thin silky threads for his web. He spun out two threads and asked each of his sons to take the end of one of the threads. Then he told Akwete to wind a thread tightly around his upper body near the neck; and Akuete to do the same around his hips. Then he sent each son to an opposite side of the forest, and told them to pull on the thread if they found the location of the festival, so he could follow the thread and join the merriment.

This is what happened. Not long afterward, the one who went to the left, Akwete, tripped over a root and, in his fall, pulled on the thread. The spider said, "Good, at last," and he laughed. "Now I can enjoy the festival," and he hurried toward the left.

But, at the same time, the one on the right, Akuete, suddenly heard the sounds of dancing and music at the festival. He grew very excited, and ran with all his speed toward the music. He was not thinking at all about his father, Ananse.

Then, while trying to stand, Akwete fell again, pulling the string even tighter. Ananse was caught in the middle of the two threads, running first one way, then the other, until finally the strings broke. It is said Ananse was almost cut into three parts. He was in great agony for many days.

After the spider's pain healed, he found his body was divided into three unequal parts. He had a tiny head and a medium sized chest and a great silly-looking stomach. And he learned that, in his next scheme, he should pick better partners.

15

The Clever Spider

One fine and sunny day the spider went to the river to fish for catfish. It was his lucky day, and he was catching fish using only his empty hook. There were so many fish swimming all around that it seemed they were jumping into his basket. Soon he had enough catfish for a meal or two.

Now a catfish is delicate and one must know how to prepare it. It has to be skinned. So the spider skinned the fish carefully and made a fire to roast his catch for the evening meal. The fish looked delicious, and one could smell it all the way to the other end of the river.

Naturally, it attracted many of the animals. But the spider refused to share his meal. As he sat down on a log

to eat, he heard a voice say, "Give me that fish if you know what is good for you."

It was the lion, who had sniffed his way from across the river. Being the king of the jungle, he shouted at the spider to deliver up his catch, for all that is in the forest belonged to the king.

"Well sir," said the Spider, "you are the fiercest of all the animals and you deserve a better meal than these measly roasted catfish."

By this time the lion was all wet in the face from the saliva dripping from his mouth. "Now let me have the fish," he said. "I am king of the jungle."

The spider was frightened, but thought fast, and suddenly started to laugh.

"Why are you laughing?" asked the lion.

"Oh, I am not laughing at you. I am just thinking of you eating these skinny fish. Look over there and see the deer— now that is a meal fit for a king. As for me, I'd rather have a king's meal than these measly fish."

And so the lion bounded off after the deer, leaving the spider to finish his fish dinner in peace. It is said that to this day the lion still chases the deer any time they meet in the forest. And that the spider still eats all his fish, and none dare challenge him.

16

How Knowledge Spread Throughout the World

This is an old story. It is a story of greed. And the spider is a good example of how greed works. It happened so long ago that some people have forgotten what happened or how it all started.

So long ago that one cannot imagine how long, as the old people say, the world spoke only one language and had only one knowledge. Everybody had access to the one knowledge and this made them all smart and happy. Well, so they thought.

But there was sadness in the spider's heart, because he thought perhaps if he had knowledge all for himself, he could make everybody pay for it one piece at a time.

Well, as the story goes, one fine day the spider collected all the knowledge in the world. It was easy then. One only has to imagine it. All knowledge in one place. The spider then put all the collected knowledge into a big gourd.

A gourd is like a small pumpkin or squash, and is hollowed out and used as a bottle, or something to drink from. It has a small neck. Even today some people keep juices fresh in gourds in Africa.

As the story continues, the spider placed the knowledge into the gourd and then tried to think where to hide it. He finally had a bright idea. He decided to climb the tallest tree in order to place the gourd full of knowledge there so that no one else could reach it.

But, as he was climbing, something happened. The spider had placed the gourd around his neck on a string, and instead of hanging on his back, it was in front of him. This got in his way as he climbed, and soon the gourd fell down and broke. And what do you think? All the collected knowledge escaped, and the wind carried it to all the corners of the world.

So men and women and children of all nations now have access to knowledge. But each person has only a fraction of it, so nobody has all knowledge. And we think that is for the best.

17

How Mountains, Hills, and Rivers Came to Be

Once upon a time in a land which no one can name and at a time no one can determine, the earth was smooth and flat and all the animals and plants lived in harmony—except for the spider, who was always trying to start a fight among those who dwell in the trees and those who walk on the forest floor. Even the earth and the sky were on good terms, and worked together for the benefit of all.

And one day the spider, who liked to cause trouble, went to the sky and told him that the earth had proclaimed that he, the earth, was the greatest of God's creations. This made the sky very angry. He challenged the earth to a contest to settle who was the greatest.

During the arguments the sky thundered and sent down rain and lightning. The earth shook and quaked and spewed fire, and opened up in places. The sky sent down more floods of water.

The animals were all afraid and fled for their lives. Some parts of the earth rose and formed mountains and valleys. The sky sent down so much water that rivers and lakes appeared.

So now we have rivers, hills and mountains. The contest between earth and sky was never completed, and even to this day, once in a while you can hear thunder and see lightning from the sky, and waters flooding the earth and chasing all the animals away.

As for the spider, he got away as always to think about his next prank.

18

The
Fox's Tail

The fox used to be a good friend of humans. That was a long, long time ago. They were at peace, and neither bothered the other. But this is all changed today. The fox hates humans because they try to hunt him down.

It all started long ago when a man made a wager with the fox. In those days the fox was the most ingenious animal of them all. He was smart and sleek. The wager was that the fox could be caught in a trap.

Unfortunately the fox lost: he got caught in the man's trap. He managed to free himself, but in doing so he left a piece of his tail behind. Naturally, the fox was incensed, since the fashion in those days did not call for foxes with short tails. But the fox conceived a

way out. (It was his character always to attempt to turn defeat into victory.) He went up to the council of foxes and told them of a new fashion among foxes that called for short tails, like his own. It sounded like a nice idea, until one smart fox asked the would-be fashion setter how he happened to get his tail cut off in the first place. Naturally, the short-tailed one could not disclose the circumstances. And that is what has saved the tails of all foxes, up to this day.

19

The Fox
and the Lion

During his travels in the forest, the fox came upon the tall grassland where the little animals live, including the lizard, the snake, the rabbit, and the squirrel, to mention just a few. He was told that, although the only lion who lived among them had gotten so old that he no longer came out of his cave, even to chase them around for food, many of the animals had mysteriously disappeared. So the fox went to see the aged and sickly king of the forest.

The ailing lion was found at the door of his cave, and when he saw the fox he began to cough and moan. Pathetic in manner and voice, he begged the fox to come inside and visit. When the fox declined, the lion said in a quavery voice, "But all the animals have come

in here to visit me because I am sick and old. You can even see their footprints." He pointed to the footprints in front of his cave.

"Oh, yes," said the fox. "I see their footprints entering the cave, all right, but the funny thing is that there are no footprints coming out—ha, ha, ha."

Then, leaping to grab the fox, the lion growled, "You nasty, sneaky, conniving fox, I'll teach you to be so smart!"

But the fox escaped, and from that day no fox has ever gone close to a lion's cave. And all animals learned a lesson, which is not to trust a sick lion.

20

Treat Others As You Would Like Them to Treat You

The stork and the fox were once very good friends. Well, that was before they became bitter enemies.

According to the story, the fox once invited the stork to dinner, and when the stork came the fox served dinner on a flat plate. Now, everybody knows that because the stork has a long beak, he can eat only from a bowl, and not from a flat plate. So the stork could not eat, and was so hungry he could have swallowed a whole shark.

Not long after this, the stork decided to teach the fox a lesson by paying him back in his own coin. He invited the fox for dinner and served delicious foods in jars with long necks. The fox could not eat, and was so

frustrated he tried to devour the stork. But the stork flew away, and has never made his home in that forest again.

21

Don't Trouble Trouble Till Trouble Troubles You

For the Accra people, it is taboo to hunt on Friday. No one knows exactly how this came about, but tradition has it that a long time ago everybody used to go out and hunt for food on any day at all, and there were no restrictions whatsoever. Then an unscrupulous man was hunting one fine Friday and found a turtle playing a guitar and singing. At that time, though animals and even trees were known to have talked to men, it was a rare occurrence. So this incident was quite unusual.

According to tradition, no one ever lived to tell about it when spoken to by an animal; so it was rather disturbing to the people when the hunter came back with the turtle and claimed that he could get the animal

to sing and play the guitar just as he had found him doing in the forest. The hunter swore an oath by the sacred shrines and by the gods of the Accra people, and upon that he was taken at his word.

All the people assembled in the public square, and in attendance were the chief of the Accra people, his sub-chiefs and their council. People came from near and far, both young and old. There was great excitement over whether the hunter could fulfill his promise.

So the time came, and the hunter was called forward. There was a sudden hush on the crowd. The square was so quiet that one could hear the rats digging miles away. Then majestically the chief rose and called on the hunter to step forward and perform his wonderful feat, but promising to cut off his head if he had fooled the people. The hunter confidently stepped forward, set the turtle in the center of the square and commanded him by the powers of the gods of the Sakumo and Klotey lagoons to sing and play his guitar. Nothing happened, however. The hunter repeated the command, but the turtle just sat there. After a while the crowd, including the chief, got tired of the performance, and the chief

pronounced a judgement of death on the hunter for not doing what he had claimed he could do.

Long after the guards had taken the hunter away, a shrill voice was heard. Everybody had forgotten the turtle; and when they looked around, it was the turtle singing and playing his guitar. And these were the words of the song he was singing:

"Don't trouble trouble till trouble troubles you."

And ever since that day the moral of the story has remained with all hunters. And for fear of meeting strange things, no hunter ever goes hunting on Friday.

22

How the Lizard
Got His Flat Head

The old folks still remember when the lizard had a round head, just like any other animal in the bush. But today the lizard's head is awkwardly flattened, and this is how it happened.

A long time ago a chief had a daughter; and when the daughter grew up, she became the most beautiful girl in all the land. But no one outside the royal household had ever seen the beautiful face or figure of this lovely princess, for according to the tradition of the time, it was taboo to gaze upon her.

Now, it happened that the daughter of the chief took a bath every day at dawn, when all the men were asleep; and only her maids in attendance knew just where. One day the lizard, who was very inquisitive,

climbed up the tall odum tree that stood behind the fence of the palace and waited there to have a peek at the daughter of the chief. Unfortunately, he had chosen the wrong tree. He waited all day, but the daughter and her servants did not arrive.

Night came, and he fell asleep. His sleep was so deep that he lost his balance and fell. And if you have ever fallen from an odum tree, you will know how it was. The lizard's fall was so hard that when he got up, his arms and legs were broken into parts.

You can still feel the broken bones of the lizard in his limbs; and his skin, which was shattered by the fall, still has a rough, scaly feeling. As for his head, it stayed flat forever. And people still comment that every time the lizard shakes his head he is trying to shake off the effects of that fall.

23

Procrastination Doesn't Pay

The earthworm was not always as he is now. In the beginning God (Nyonmo) the Creator bid all the animals to come get their eyes when He had finished creating the rest of them. But the earthworm replied, "I don't need to see now. I will wait until I grow up before I come for my eyes." And so he did. But when he finally went to God for his eyes, God had none left for him. He had given all the available eyes away.

The earthworm is still blind and burrows in the soil. Some say he lost his eyes and is looking for them. But the old ones know what really happened. This is why children are always advised by the old ones not to put off till tomorrow what can be done today.

24

Why the
Tortoise's Shell Is Cracked

Children always wonder why there are cracks in the tortoise's shell. Well, it all happened like this (and according to the old people, it is a true story):

The tortoise was once a good friend of the vulture. The vulture always came to visit the tortoise, and not the other way around, because he could fly and the tortoise could not. The poor tortoise not only could not fly; even his walking was very slow and laborious.

The situation seemed to belittle the tortoise, who became concerned that he could not go over to visit the vulture. This, the tortoise thought, might eventually offend his friend. So, one day the tortoise talked it over with his wife, and he asked her to wrap him in a parcel,

which she was to give to the vulture as a gift on his next visit. The next day the vulture tried to visit the tortoise as usual. He did not stay long, because his friend was not home. But the tortoise's wife told him that her husband had left a parcel for him to take back. The vulture was not to open it until he got home. This was the tortoise's way of surprising his friend with a visit. So the vulture picked up the parcel and flew away.

Soon the tortoise felt like scratching, and as he scratched it tickled the feet of the vulture. This caused the vulture to let the parcel go, and it fell down with the tortoise inside it. The fall was so hard that it cracked the tortoise's shell.

When the vulture discovered his friend the tortoise had tricked him, he became angry and flew away, and the tortoise, with his back full of cracks, had to walk back home. It was a long, slow journey, and the tortoise had plenty of time to think about how his friend was a vulture who could soar high in the sky, and that he was a tortoise who crawled slowly across the ground. But, perhaps that was the way it was meant to be. And that is why the old people say how much wiser it is to accept things as they are, instead of trying to change what cannot be changed.

25

The Two Caterpillars

Two caterpillars were crawling across the grass when a butterfly flew over them. One nudged the other and said, "You couldn't get me up there for all the money in the world. I belong on the ground, and here I will stay."

But the other one said, "Crawling on the ground is not my true nature. One day I will be up there where the birds are."

And so he went through life until finally one day he changed, to become a beautiful butterfly with strong wings and many bright and shiny colors.

But the other one stayed a caterpillar, crawling around and eating leaves all his life because he never

dared to be anything else. He did not know his true self. And only those who know their true selves can soar like the butterfly.